OTTER ON HIS OWN
The Story of a Sea Otter

SMITHSONIAN OCEANIC COLLECTION

For my father and mother, who share my love for the sea. — D.B.

To Nicole, Dana, and Nicholas. — L.B.

Book Design: Shields & Partners, Westport, CT

First Edition 1995
10 9
Printed in China

Acknowledgments:
   Soundprints would like to thank Dr. Charles Handley of the Department of Vertebrate Zoology at the Smithsonian Institution's National Museum of Natural History for his curatorial review.
   The author thanks the following individuals for their input: Ellen Faurot-Daniels, Dina Stansbury and Susan Brown from Friends of the Sea Otter in Carmel, California; LeAnn Gast and Dennis Maroulas from the Aquarium for Wildlife Conservation in New York City; and Daniel, Spanky, Elsa and Bunky, a "raft" of southern sea otters rehabilitated at Monterey Bay Aquarium and now residents of Coney Island, New York.

OTTER ON HIS OWN
The Story of a Sea Otter

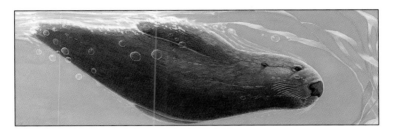

by Doe Boyle   Illustrated by Lisa Bonforte

Soundprints
Where Children Discover Nature

In a sheltered cove at the edge of the great Pacific Ocean, Sea Otter Pup and his mother lie cradled in a golden-brown bed of giant kelp. The foghorn echoes from the rocky point as the morning mist rises.

Like a wooly ball, Pup rests on his mother's chest. He is two hours old, and today is his first day on the sea.

The sunshine of late winter warms the rocky California shore, but the water is cold. Sea Otter Pup's loose fur protects him like cozy pajamas. Mother keeps his fur clean and dry, rubbing it between her forepaws and blowing warm air into it with her mouth and nose.

Mother is hungry. She plucks Pup from her belly and plops him on the surface of the sea. She drapes a smooth ribbon of kelp across his belly to anchor him. Pup bobs up and down on the waves like a cork. Then, Mother dives below to forage for her dinner.

Pup shrieks for his missing mother. He hears only the sounds of the other otter pups and mothers in the cove.

Up pops Mother! She coos at Pup and props him up on her belly. Pup watches curiously as Mother pulls the soft meat from a sea urchin she has found in the forest of kelp.

When she is done, she rolls and tumbles in the water to clean her fur. Pup tries to tumble with her, but he is too young. He scolds his twirling mother with a piercing wail, and she comes to play with him in the waves.

For several months, Pup shares his mother's food. Mother breaks the hard shells of clams, abalone and urchins on rocks she finds on the ocean floor.

Crack! Crack! The sound of her pounding carries above the cries of the hovering gulls who wait to steal fallen morsels.

By springtime, Otter Pup is sleek and strong.
He can swim and somersault like his mother.
He is eager to search the world beneath the
waves for his own dinner. It is time for his
first dive.

With a great who-oo-sh of bubbles,
Pup rolls forward and pushes downward
with his webbed hind feet.

Pup has not pushed hard enough!
He grabs a frond of kelp to pull
himself to the sandy bottom.

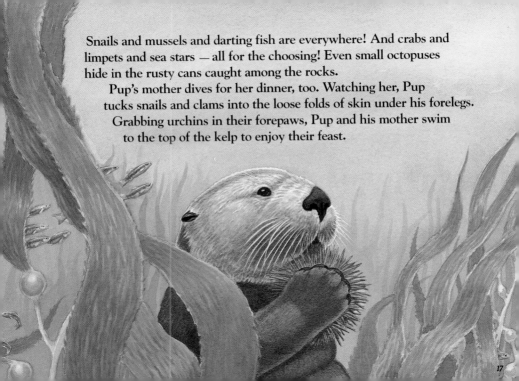

Snails and mussels and darting fish are everywhere! And crabs and limpets and sea stars — all for the choosing! Even small octopuses hide in the rusty cans caught among the rocks.

Pup's mother dives for her dinner, too. Watching her, Pup tucks snails and clams into the loose folds of skin under his forelegs. Grabbing urchins in their forepaws, Pup and his mother swim to the top of the kelp to enjoy their feast.

Floating on his back, Pup spreads his dinner on his belly and tears at an urchin. He snorts and sniffs, plucking snail treasure from his "pocket." Sometimes he picks out pebbles he has taken by mistake.

Throughout the warm days of spring, Otter Pup perfects his hunting and diving. He learns to pry the stubborn abalone from the rocks below. After each dive and every meal, he grooms himself carefully. Bits of his food or oil from the huge ships that pass offshore can mat his thick fur. He keeps each hair spotlessly clean.

One afternoon Pup's mother leaves the cove to look for squid. Pup is curious. Following her beyond the rocky point, Pup feels the powerful breath of the ocean on his whiskers. Under the choppy swells, Pup hears new sounds — the chirps and whistles of dolphins, the whir and thunder of boats. He cannot see or hear his mother.

Pup calls, but Mother does not answer. When he spots her among the waves, it is too late. A silent creature streaks by him. The great white shark hurls Pup's mother high above the salty spray with a tremendous shake. Screaming, she slams down into the water and disappears.

Pup cries and frantically searches the water for his mother.
Suddenly, Pup feels a rough tug at his forepaw. Frightened, he whirls
about, but the vicious shark is gone, searching for tastier prey.
Mother is at his side, pushing him toward the safety of the kelp.
They race forward until the gentle kelp encircles them.
Tonight there will be no diving. Rocking side by side,
Mother and Pup sleep.

At dawn, the cove is foggy and quiet, except for the bellow of the foghorn. Pup's bruised mother feeds lazily on the snails in the kelp canopy, while Pup dives alone for the sweet, pink flesh of abalone.

By summer's end, Otter Pup is
almost fully grown. The world beyond
the cove is full of danger, but Otter is filled
with a new curiosity and restlessness.

One morning Otter leaves his mother. Out
past the rocky point, out past the foghorn, he swims.
Today is Otter's first day on his own.

About the Sea Otter

One of the smallest marine mammals, sea otters live close to the Pacific coast in waters about 30 to 50 feet deep. Sea otter pups usually stay with their mothers for six to nine months, often with other otters in a group called a raft. Sea otters have the densest fur of any creature on earth, with up to a million hairs per square inch. This hair traps air bubbles, insulating them against the cold water.

Sea otters eat many invertebrates, which are animals without backbones. Among them are abalone, whose shells sea otters crack open with rocks. This behavior makes sea otters one of the few tool-using animals. They are also able to pry open submerged cans with their teeth to eat the young octopuses that live inside.

Sea otters came close to extinction during The Great Hunt that began in 1743. In 1911, they gained protection under a law that prohibited otter hunting and the sale of otter pelts. Even though sea otters have increased in numbers, hazards created by humans keep their survival in question.

Glossary

abalone: A rock-hugging mollusk that clings to surfaces with a large, muscular "foot."

forage: To hunt for food by searching, browsing or grazing.

giant kelp: A fast-growing greenish-brown seaweed that flourishes along the California coast. Kelp forests attach to rocks on the sea bottom and grow to the surface, forming beds. Their long branches, or fronds, are kept afloat by small balloon-like bladders.

great white shark: A fierce and dangerous species of shark with three-inch teeth.

limpet: A mollusk with a conical shell that clings tightly to rocks.

sea urchin: A round invertebrate with a thin, brittle shell covered with movable spines.

squid: A marine animal with a long tapered body and ten arms.

webbed: Having skin between the toes for extra swimming power.